The Mystery Of The UFOs

Written
By
SARAH CHIN

Archway Publishing books may be ordered through booksellers or by contacting:

Archway Publishing
1663 Liberty Drive
Bloomington, IN 47403
www.archwaypublishing.com
844-669-3957

Interior Image Credit: Momina Iqbal

ISBN: 978-1-6657-1212-5 (sc)
ISBN: 978-1-6657-1213-2 (e)

Print information available on the last page.

Archway Publishing rev. date: 10/01/2021

Once upon a time, there was a girl named Iris who had a brother named Aaron.

Iris and Aaron did their chores, but when they were finished, they played in the garden.

Iris and Aaron always fed the chickens as one of their chores. One day, Iris noticed all the plants they had just watered disappeared, and suddenly ten-foot-wide circles appeared in the garden patch. "Um, Aaron, what are those circles?" asked Iris.

"Oh, uh, I mean, I don't know," admitted Aaron. He didn't like it when he didn't know the stuff that others didn't know either.

Iris sensed his sadness and gave him a friendly smile. "It's OK not to know stuff," she told Aaron. "Maybe there's an answer in the library."

"Yeah, you're right. Last week I was confused with my math, and I went to the library and found a great answer that helped me solve it," said Aaron.

"Then let's go to the library!" said Iris.

Iris and Aaron walked to the library and soon they were there.

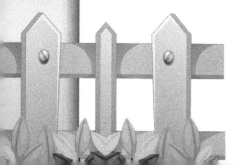

"No, not yet. You?" asked Aaron.

"No," said Iris. "Wait, Aaron."

"Yes?" said Aaron.

"Look," said Iris. "This picture looks just like our garden this morning. The book says those circles were created by UFOs. Aaron, maybe we should find out what UFOs are."

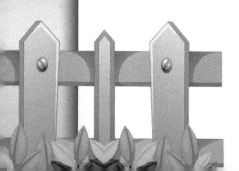

"OK, good idea, Iris," said Aaron.

Back at home, they picked up two sticks, some avocado leaves, some rocks, and some water. Then they set the sticks down, put the leaves over them, and piled the rocks on top.

"OK, pour the water, Aaron!" shouted Iris.

Aaron poured the water, and then he and Iris waited. But nothing happened. Iris let out a sigh.

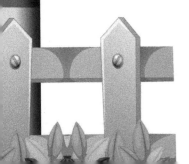
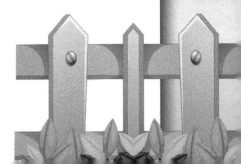

"Hi, Iris! Hi, Aaron!" said Emily.

"What are you doing?" asked Harry.

"We are trying to find out what UFOs are," said Aaron.

"Wow! Cool! Can we help?" asked Emily.

"OK, then," said Iris.

They went to Iris and Aaron's garden and grabbed what they needed.

"I'm gonna take a video," said Emily. Her grandma had bought a camera for her on her birthday.

"Emily, we're here to help, not to take a video," said Harry gently.

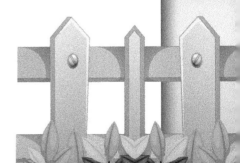

But Emily didn't listen.

"Harry, can you lend me a hand on this one?" grunted Aaron, trying to dig.

"Sure thing, Aaron!" Harry said cheerfully.

You pull the shovel handle and I'll lift. Three, two, one, *pull*!" said Aaron.

"Argh!" screamed Harry as dirt flew to his face.

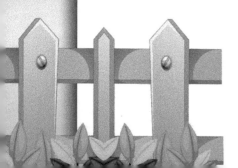

"I'll take a bath when I get home." He stiffened when Emily giggled.

"Are you OK?" asked Iris.

"No, I am not OK!" shouted Harry.

"What is wrong with you today?" yelled Emily.

"Me! What is wrong with *you* today?" he yelled back. As the two bickered, Iris and Aaron just shrugged and went back to work.

"I've had enough! I'm going home!" shouted Emily furiously. She and her brother stormed off.

Awhile later, Harry and Emily came back, this time with smiling faces. Then Iris saw their other friends Terria and Henry.

"Welcome back, guys!" said Aaron.

"Can we let Terria and Henry help too?" asked Emily.

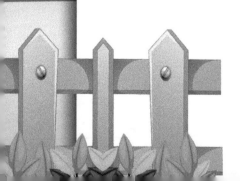

They poured the dirt on wet cement and grass, put grass on water and dirt, put cobwebs in the cement, and added leaves on paper and paste to the top. But whatever they tried, nothing worked.

"It's useless," said Iris sadly.

Aaron hung his head.

"What do we do now?" said Harry.

Emily and Henry sighed together.

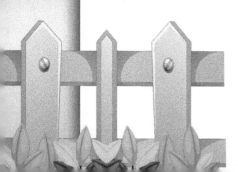

But Terria didn't look upset. She touched Iris's arm and said, "It's not too late, everyone. We can solve the mystery if we never give up!"

Terria, Henry, Iris, Aaron, Harry, and Emily all took deep breaths.

Iris said, "Yes, you are right, Terria. Not giving up is the answer. We must use teamwork!"

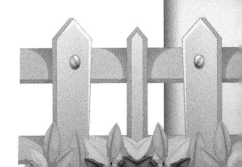

"I feel much better already," said Aaron.

"And stronger," added Emily.

"I feel great!" said Harry.

"Wait a second. What we've been doing ... well, it doesn't make sense. It should be a mixture of dirt, water, and sun to make it feels like clay then it'll look like a shape of an UFO," said Terria. She paused for a moment or so and then said, "Yeah. Yeah, that does make sense!"

Terria grinned shyly. "I found a book last week saying some UFOs are caused by dirt, water, and sun," Terria answered.

"Sorry, Terria, but despite everything you mentioned, we'll go with my idea first, then Aaron's, Harry's, and Emily's ideas. But mine's first," said Iris.

Terria sighed. *Why do they always do that?* she thought.

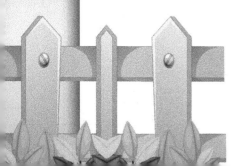

But Aaron nodded. "Yeah, I think you're right, Iris."

Harry nodded too. "I agree."

"OK," said Emily.

Henry hung his head. "Sorry, sis," said Henry. "They like Iris's idea better than yours."

"No, no. Don't apologize. It's not your fault," said Terria. "I'll just let them try and then see who's right.

"You sure?"

"I'm sure."

So that's what they did. Iris's idea didn't work, and neither did Aaron's, Harry's, or Emily's.

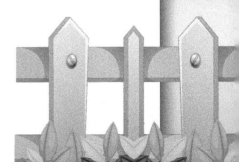

"And that's why I think you're the best brother a sister like me could ask for. You always speak up for me," said Terria gratefully.

"Awww! Thanks, sis!" said Henry.

The six friends tried Terria's idea—and for a few seconds, it worked!

"Look, look! It worked!" cried Iris.

"Hooray!" cried Aaron.

"Sorry we didn't trust you, Terria," said Harry.

"We'll trust you from now on!" said Emily.

"A high-five promise to the smartest girl in the world!" said Henry.

"This is a day I'll never forget," said Terria.

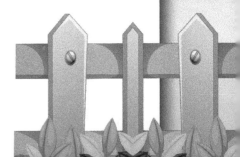

The End

CPSIA information can be obtained
at www.ICGtesting.com
Printed in the USA
LVHW051101301021
701900LV00004B/12